This book was made possible due to the
generous funding of Derrick Cresswell-Clough
and 110 Kickstarter Backers.
Thank you!

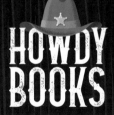

HOWDY
BOOKS

by

red barn
- BOOKS -

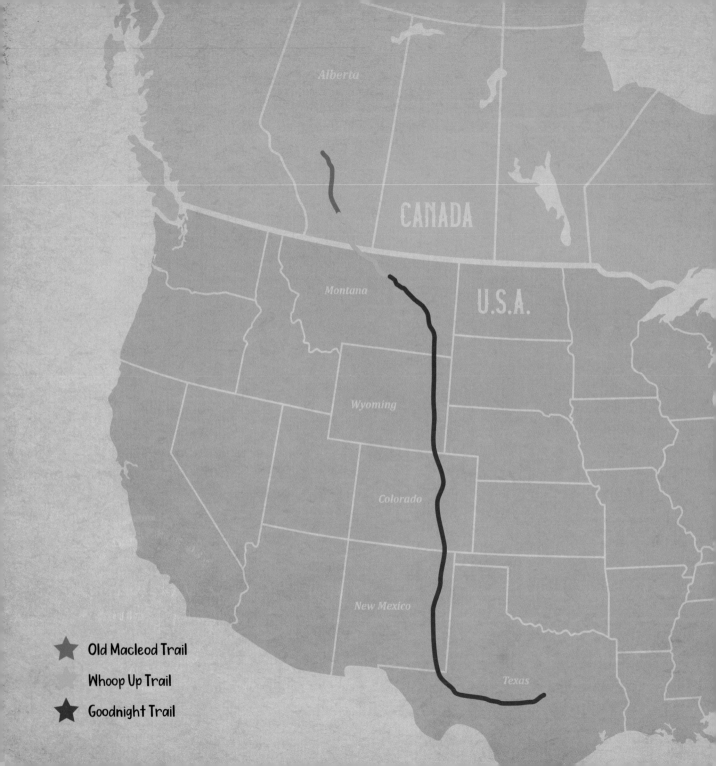

Old Macleod Trail

Whoop Up Trail

Goodnight Trail

HOWDY, I'M JOHN WARE

And this is the story of my cowboy life.

Written by Ayesha Clough ★ Illustrated by Hugh Rookwood
Edited by Frank Dabbs ★ Designed by Lia Golemba

I was born a long time ago, round about 1850. My family was enslaved in the southern United States.

Some say I grew up on a cotton plantation in Tennessee or South Carolina.

6

Others say we lived on a ranch in Texas.

I don't like to talk about this time.

Terrible things happened. Black people were bought and sold in markets, like animals. Our 'masters' worked us hard, and beat us often.

Then came the American Civil War, four years of fighting between North and South. The North won in 1865. The country was re-united, and slavery was made illegal everywhere in the US.

11

The trail was rough. I was a 'drag man', stuck at the back with my friend Bill Moodie, breathing in the dust of two thousand unruly critters.

Next up, in 1882, was a cattle drive from Idaho to Alberta, Canada. We got paid a dollar a day plus grub.

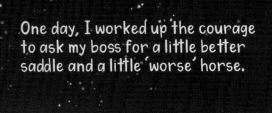

One day, I worked up the courage to ask my boss for a little better saddle and a little 'worse' horse.

FINALLY. GOT ME A LIVE ONE!

IF BY WORSE, YOU MEAN WILDER, WE HAVE A REAL BAD BRONC FOR YOU.

IF YOU CAN RIDE HIM, YOU CAN KEEP HIM.

YAAAAAHOOOOOOOOO

I rode that bronc to a standstill. And I kept him.

Soon I was riding by day, alongside the best cowboys, at the front of the herd.

17

When we got to Alberta, Fred Stimson offered me a job at the Bar U Ranch, south of Millarville. I jumped at it.

Soon, the **LEGENDS ABOUT ME** began to grow.

He was **STRUCK BY LIGHTNING** and he lived

He can **RIDE ANYTHING** with hair on!

He can **LIFT** a small **COW**

He can **WALK** across a cattle pen on the **BACKS OF BULLS**

He's hands-down the **BEST** rider and roper **IN THE WEST**

He can **WRESTLE A STEER** to the ground

It's true I was big and strong. But here's my secret. I connected with animals. Like me, they had to work for a master. But there was no need for fear and violence.

I cared about them, showed them love and respect. They, in turn, gave their best for me.

Mildred was a wonderful wife. She handled the ranch accounts and read me the papers, because I couldn't read or write. She even milked cows and sold butter!

31

Settlers were building homes near Millarville. It was getting crowded. I needed lots of grass for my growing herd.

So, in 1900, we moved to Duchess, north of Brooks, in the Alberta Badlands.

That year, the Red Deer River flooded. Our cabin was washed away.

But ranchers don't know the meaning of the word **quit**.

I built us a new home on higher ground. In time,
Mildred and I had five beautiful children, and a
thousand of the finest range cattle.

I couldn't have asked for a better life, out here in God's country.

I died doing what **I loved** – riding my horse, tending cattle, on my very own ranch.

My gentle mare tripped in a badger hole and fell on me. Boom, I was gone.

Can you believe it? After all the wild broncs I'd ridden, my own sweet girl did me in!

It was a fitting end for this old cowboy, in Canada, my chosen country, and Alberta, my adopted home.

My funeral in Calgary was the largest that young city had ever seen. Ranchers came from miles and miles to say goodbye to me, their old friend and neighbour.

JOHN WITH HIS BOARHOUND
BISMARK, 1891

JOHN AND
MILDRED'S
MARRIAGE
CERTIFICATE,
1892

WARE RANCH NEAR MILLARVILLE, 1896

PHOTOS +TIMELINE

1850
Born in
Southern US.

1882
Brings first cattle
to District of
Alberta in the
NW Territories.

1884
Railway brings settlers to
Alberta. Calgary becomes
a town, population 500.

1888
Builds cabin
at Millarville.

WITH NETTIE AND BABY
ROBERT, 1896

Photos courtesy of Glenbow Archives, Archives and Special Collections, University of Calgary. Modifications to the images include colour correction and cropping.

1900
Moves to Brooks.

1892
Marries Mildred.
Railway expands,
opening up farmland.

1894
Calgary becomes a city,
population 3,900.

1905
Alberta becomes a province.
John and Mildred pass away
within months of each other.

Notes for Educators

Prepared by Laurel Scharien,
B.A, B.Ed., Instructional Designer

The enduring story of John Ware's courage, vision and kindness is a springboard for countless educational experiences. The story of a man finding a community and his own identity, *Howdy, I'm John Ware* is a valuable narrative for learners in Alberta and beyond.

This book offers students the opportunity to explore his unique perspective as an Alberta settler, and why we should strive to understand and accept people of different backgrounds.

Students can empathize with his courage, fears and kindness as he becomes a cowboy and pioneer rancher, in his quest for a better quality of life. Students can analyze the value of these changes and compare Ware's journey to a variety of present-day experiences.

Ware's need for large areas of grassland to feed his cattle causes him to relocate his ranch to a less settled area. Students can examine his relationship with the land, consider the perspective of incoming settlers and analyze his decision to relocate.

Readers will appreciate the contributions he made to his new community and Alberta's nascent cattle industry. Through shared experiences with fellow cowboys and settlers, Ware was given something in return. His identity changed from a slave to a successful ranch owner.

This story can be used to develop literacy, conceptual knowledge and procedural knowledge in numerous ways. A few examples follow that are tailored to Alberta's Program of Studies for Grades Four to Seven. Educators can explore other topics such as slavery in the US and Canada, racism, Alberta's pioneer women, history of ranching and cattle brands, settlement of the Canadian West, and shaping of a Western identity.

 ## CRITICAL THINKING

Explore the perspectives of John and the various people he encounters, and what may be influencing their opinions of one another.

Brainstorm attributes of a good friend. Would John Ware be a good friend? Why?

CREATIVE THINKING

Brainstorm alternative endings to the story. If John hadn't had an accident, what might he have gone on to accomplish in his life? (leadership roles, innovative discoveries…)

Examine 'helpfulness' and discuss ways John contributed to his community. Do you think John would be helpful if he lived in our community today? How?

HISTORIC THINKING

What was life like for Alberta's pioneer ranchers? What day-to-day challenges did they face?

Pretend you are a newcomer who wants to start your own cattle ranch, like John did. How would you go about it?

GEOGRAPHIC THINKING

How did Alberta's physical geography and natural environment both sustain and challenge life for Alberta's early ranchers? Compare the unique geography of the Canadian Badlands region with the rest of Southern Alberta.

Imagine John decided to stay and ranch near Millarville. You are a new settler in the area and you need land and water, but the cattle are EVERYWHERE. Write John a letter about how this is affecting your farm.

DECISION MAKING & PROBLEM SOLVING

List the pros and cons of John's decision to move his ranch to Duchess (feed and water for his animals, flood risk, access to schools and medical care …)

On the cattle drive to Alberta, John faced discrimination in many forms, ranging from being tasked with simple, menial jobs to being given an inferior horse and saddle. How would you react – if you were John, or if you were his friend Bill Moodie?

LEARN AND EXPLORE!

- Watch the John Ware video by the Rella Black History Foundation, and read Natasha Henry's report.
- Go see the beautifully preserved Ware cabin at Dinosaur Provincial Park near Brooks.
- Tour the Bar U Ranch National Historic Site near Longview, where John once worked.
- Visit Mackay Cabin in Heritage Park's Settlement area, where it's believed Nettie Ware was born.
- See the Glenbow Museum's Mavericks Exhibit, and search their online 'John Ware, Lewis Family Fonds'. Read *John Ware's Cow Country* by Grant MacEwan (1960) in their Digital Collection.
- Visit the Stockmen's Memorial Foundation in Cochrane, the Highwood Museum in High River, and the Vulcan Museum, and ask to see their Ware and Lewis family archives.
- Find John and Mildred's graves at Union Cemetery in Calgary.
- Listen to the CBC News podcasts about John Ware.
- Watch the NFB Documentary called *John Ware Reclaimed* by Cheryl Foggo.

SOURCES

- *John Ware's Cow Country* by Grant MacEwan (UCalgary Digital Collection, 1960)
- Ware and Lewis Family Fonds at the Glenbow, Highwood and Stockmen's Museums (Calgary and Area, 2019-20)
- Interviews with historian Cheryl Foggo (Calgary, 2019-20)

DEAR READER

We've tried to make this book as accurate as we can. It's difficult because historical records are hard to find, and John didn't know how to write. So we rely on news archives and accounts from his friends, and most importantly, Janet 'Nettie' Ware, his eldest child. But Nettie was only 12 when John died, and she didn't recall her father speaking about his early years.

The great irony of John's story is that this seemingly indestructible man was killed by his gentle horse. According to Nettie, her father was never the same after he lost Mildred in the spring of 1905 to typhoid and pneumonia. You could say John died of a broken heart just months after his beloved Milly. But you can also say he lived a full and happy life – one we remember and celebrate to this day.

After their parents passed, the five Ware children were raised by their grandparents in Blairmore, Alberta. None of John's kids had children, so sadly, he has no direct descendants.

THANK YOU

To Hugh Rookwood and Lia Golemba for their art and creative vision. To Tyler Dixon for the story outline, and Frank Dabbs for his big thinking. To Lee and Mike McLean of High River, and Calgary historian Cheryl Foggo for reviewing the manuscripts. To the Glenbow, Stockmen's and Highwood museums for historical treasures. To our 111 Kickstarter backers. To my family for their love and support. To Dek, my inspiration - Ayesha

Printed in Canada.
ISBN 978-1-9991087-8-6
Text © Ayesha Cresswell-Clough 2020
Illustrations © Hugh Rookwood 2020
Book design by Lia Golemba, Pink Spot Studios
Text set in My Dear Watson,
Amber Whiskey, CrimeFighter

red barn
- BOOKS -

Red Barn Books 🐷 redbarnbooks.ca.
Carstairs, Alberta, Canada.
#HowdyBooks #JohnWare

Alberta

British
Columbia

★ Edmonton

Red Deer ★

★ Cochrane
Calgary ★
★ Millarville
High River ★   Brooks ★

★ Fort Macleod

Ayesha Clough

Ayesha is a former news reporter and editor.
She began publishing books in 2019 for her
cowboy-crazy son, Derrick #4. She lives in a blue
shed in Carstairs with one hound, two horses,
and Derricks 3 and 4.

Hugh Rookwood

Hugh is a comic book artist who, from the
time he could hold a pencil, has loved to draw.
Hugh mentors young artists and travels the
world sharing his art, book covers and game
development work. He lives in Airdrie with his
wife, two sons, and Cintiq drawing tablet.